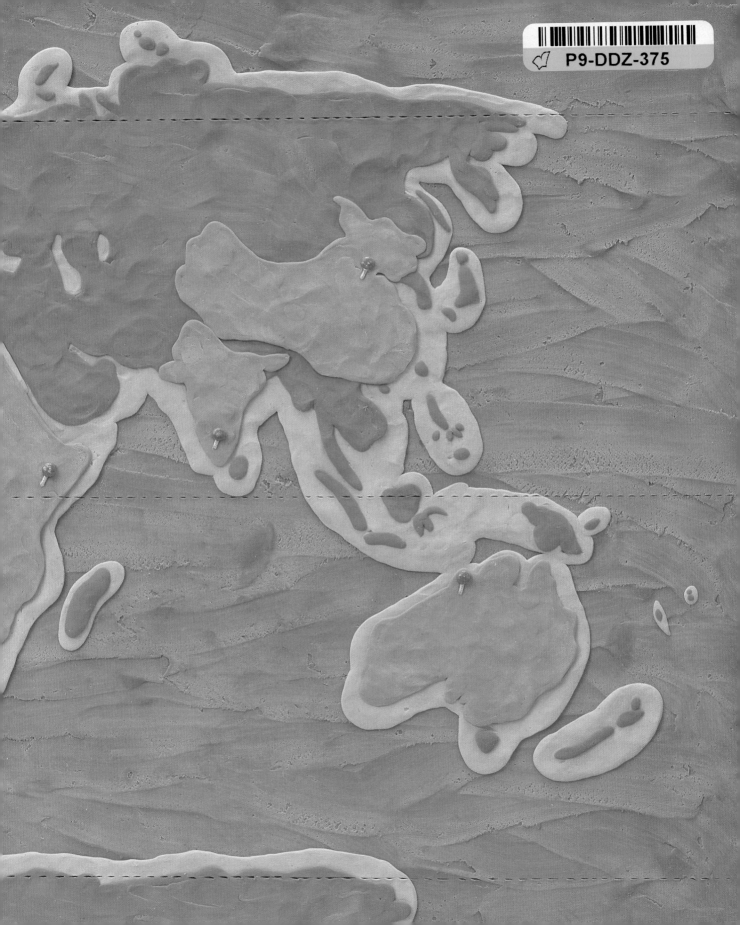

GIFTS

Jo Ellen Bogart

Barbara Reid

North Winds Press
A Division of Scholastic Canada Ltd.

The illustrations for this book were made with Plasticine
that was shaped and pressed onto illustration board.
Acrylic glaze or paint was used for shiny effects.

Photography by Ian Crysler

Canadian Cataloguing in Publication Data

Bogart, Jo Ellen, 1945 -
Gifts
ISBN 0-590-24177-X
I. Reid, Barbara, 1957- . II. Title.
PS8553.0465G5 1994   jC811'.54 C93-094776-2
PZ8.3.B64G; 1994

6 5 4 3 2   Printed in Canada   5 6 7 8/9

To the memories of my grandmothers,
Grace Ellen and Lillian Pearl.
J.E.B.

To my grandparents,
in memory of all the gifts and grab bags.
B.R.

My grandma went a-travelling,
said: "What would you have me bring?"

"Not much," said I,
"Just a piece of the sky,
and a hundred songs I can sing."

My grandma went to Africa,
said: "What would you have me bring?"

"Just a baobab seed —
that's all I need,

and a roar from the jungle king."

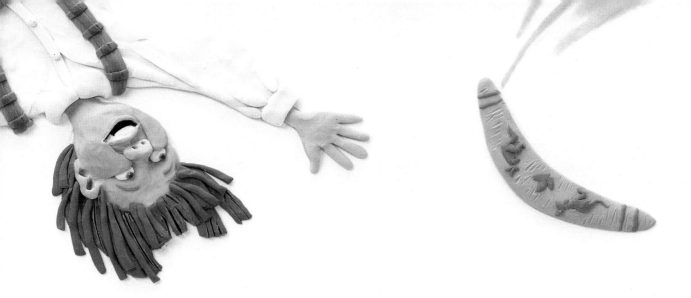

My grandma went to Australia,
said: "What would you have me bring?"

"Just a didgeridoo,
some billabong goo,
and a boomerang I can fling."

My grandma went to Mexico,
said: "What would you have me bring?"

"Just a sunrise kissed
by the morning mist,

and the whirr of a hummingbird's wing."

My grandma went to Hawaii,
said: "What would you have me bring?"

"Just the secret wish
of a flying fish,
and a rainbow to wear as a ring."

My grandma went
    to the Arctic,
said: "What would you
    have me bring?"

"Just a long white hair
from a polar bear,

and an iceberg on a string."

My grandma went to India,
said: "What would you have me bring?"

"Just something nice
like curry and rice,
and a sitar's twang and zing."

My grandma went to Switzerland,
said: "What would you have me bring?"

"Just a chunk of cheese
and a mountain, please,
and a bell that goes ding-a-ling-ling."

23

My grandma went to China,
said: "What would you have me bring?"

"Just something small
from beside the Great Wall,

and a memory from Beijing."

My grandma went to England,
said: "What would you have me bring?"

"Just the smell of rain
from a shady lane,
and a ride on a garden swing."

My gran had such a wonderful time,
that now we are going, too.
And everything she gave to me,
I'm going to give to you.

31